ANNUAL 2009

This Annual belongs to

COLLIN

Contents

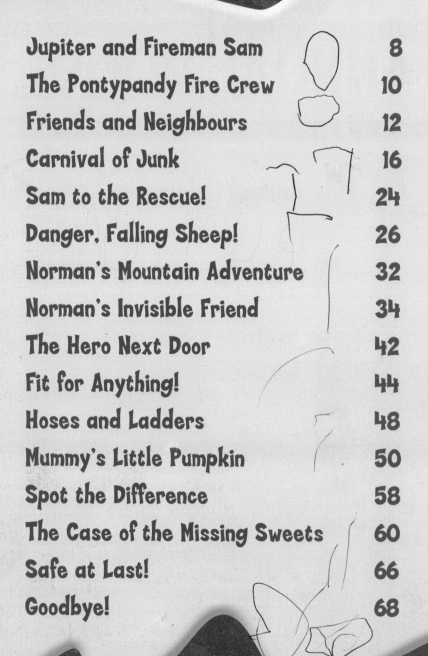

EGMONT
We bring stories to life

First published in Great Britain in 2008 by Egmont UK Limited, 239 Kensington High Street, London W8 6SA

Fireman Sam © 2008 Prism Art & Design Limited, a HIT Entertainment company. The Fireman Sam name and character are trademarks. Based on an idea by D. Gingell, D. Jones and characters created by R. M. J. Lee.

ISBN 978 1 4052 3918 9
10 9 8 7 6 5 4 3 2 1
Printed in Italy

Jupiter and Fireman Sam

Nee Nah!

This is **Jupiter**, the big red fire engine that you'll find at Pontypandy fire station.

When people see Jupiter's flashing blue lights and hear the siren, they know that help is on its way. Jupiter is always clean and shiny, and carries everything the crew needs for the rescue operation, like hoses, ladders and cutting gear.

Our Hero

Fireman Sam has the very important job of driving Jupiter.

Sam is very brave and always cool and calm in an emergency. He knows how to deal with all kinds of rescues from cats stuck up trees to big house fires.

Everyone in Pontypandy knows Fireman Sam. He's a good neighbour and a good friend, and that's why people call him the hero next door!

The Pontypandy Fire Crew

Station Officer Steele is in charge of the Pontypandy Fire Station. He's very proud of his team of firefighters, and likes them to be fit for anything, as you'll find out in the story on page 44.

"Action Stations!"

Penny Morris is a great mechanic, so if anything goes wrong with the emergency vehicles, she can fix them. She loves outdoor sports like rock climbing.

Penny drives **Venus**, the special rescue tender, which carries all the specialist gear the team needs.

Nee Nah! Nee Nah!

The rescue helicopter, Wallaby One, is stationed at the Mountain Rescue Centre on Pontypandy Mountain. Its pilot is Tom Thomas, who comes from Australia.

"Wallaby One, over and out!"

Tom also drives the bright yellow Mountain Rescue jeep.

Beep, beep!

Elvis Cridlington is the fire station cook. He's much better at firefighting than cooking – his dishes are usually disasters!

"You don't like burnt salad?"

Friends and Neighbours

Trevor Evans drives the Pontypandy bus. He takes the children to and from school, and collects and delivers things.

Parp, parp!

The **Pontypandy café** is where everyone goes to meet up with friends. They always get a warm welcome from the owner, **Bella Lasagne**, who makes great pizzas.

"Mamma mia!"

Bella's cat is called **Rosa**. She's always getting stuck up trees or down holes!

"Meow!"

There's only one grocery shop in Pontypandy. **Dilys Price** owns it, and she and her son, Norman, live in a flat above the shop.

"Norman, is that you?"

Most people call **Norman Price** Naughty Norman because he loves playing tricks and jokes! Read about his invisible friend on page 34.

"Na-naa-na-na-naa!"

Norman's pet sheep is called **Woolly**. He's not allowed in the flat, but Norman tries to get him in without his mam knowing!

"Baa, baa!"

Friends and Neighbours

Nurse Helen Flood uses her little white car, with its green cross and flashing light, to visit patients and travel to accidents.

"I'll be right there!"

Mike Flood, Helen's husband, does odd jobs, and helps at the Mountain Rescue Centre.

"I'm happy to help."

Mandy Flood is Norman's best friend. They love having adventures together.

"Let's go!"

James and **Sarah** are twins, and their uncle is Fireman Sam! You can read about when James skated into trouble and Sarah took charge on page 16.

You can read about when James skated into trouble and Sarah took charge on page 16.

"Let's play knights!"

Dusty is a stray dog, but he is well taken care of. He loves burying bones all over Pontypandy!

"Woof, woof!"

Carnival of Junk

One morning, Mike and Helen Flood were sitting down to breakfast. They were talking about going on holiday to Jamaica.

But when Mandy walked into the kitchen, they stopped talking, and stared. Her face was covered in **big red spots!**

Helen is the Pontypandy nurse, so she knew what the spots meant! "You've got chickenpox, Mandy," she said. "You'll have to stay at home for at least two weeks."

"But what about our holiday in Jamaica?" said Mandy. "That means I won't be able to go to the big carnival!"

"I know," said Helen. "It's a shame, but we'll just have to cancel the holiday and go next year, instead."

"Oh, it's not fair!" said Mandy, sadly.

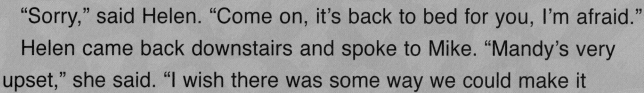

"Sorry," said Helen. "Come on, it's back to bed for you, I'm afraid."

Helen came back downstairs and spoke to Mike. "Mandy's very upset," she said. "I wish there was some way we could make it up to her."

Mike thought for a second or two. "There is!" he said. "If we can't take Mandy to the carnival, we'll bring the carnival to Mandy!"

He got out his mobile phone and rang the café.

"Hello, Bella, Mike here," he said. "Do you know any Caribbean recipes? You do? Fantastic!"

That afternoon, Sarah and James went to visit Fireman Sam
at the fire station. He was with Penny and Elvis, trying out a new
metal-cutter called the Jaws of Life.

"Fancy a game of football, Uncle Sam?" asked Sarah.

Before Sam could reply, Station Officer Steele shook his head.
"No football for your Uncle Sam today," he told the twins. "He's
much too busy here. Now off you go, you two, and find something
useful to do!"

"We will!" said James, and they rode off on their skateboards.

James went round a corner and skidded straight into a big pile of junk. There were bin bags, bits of broken furniture, and even a rusty old boiler.

"**What a mess!**" said James. "Someone must have dumped all this junk here."

"I think we've found something useful to do," said Sarah. "We can tidy it all up!"

"Good idea," said James. He pulled at a bag, but as he tugged, the big boiler rocked, bounced down, and knocked him over!

"**Ow!**" said James. "My leg's stuck under the boiler!"

"Don't move, James," said Sarah. "Your leg might be broken. I'll go to Bella's café and ring for help."

Meanwhile, Mandy was still in bed, reading a pony magazine. She didn't know that her mum and dad were making plans – carnival plans!

The other villagers were helping, too. Trevor and Norman were making balloons into animal shapes, and Bella was stirring a big pot of rice and peas.

Suddenly, Sarah ran in. "Can I use your phone, please, Bella?" she said. "It's an emergency!"

"**Mamma Mia!** Whas-a 'appen?" said Bella.

Sarah didn't have time to explain, and dialled 999. "Fire service, please!" she said. "**Hurry!**"

At the fire station, Penny read the message on the teleprinter. "Stand by, everyone!" she said. "A boy is stuck under a boiler."

"**Great Fires of London!**" said Sam. "Who is it?"

"It's James!" said Penny.

"**Action Stations!**" said Station Officer Steele.

Sam, Steele and Elvis put on their helmets and jumped on board Jupiter. The blue lights flashed, the siren wailed – **Nee Nah! Nee Nah!** – and they raced off. Penny was right behind them in Venus.

When they reached James, Dusty was looking after him!

Sam and Penny used the Jaws of Life to cut the big boiler into smaller pieces, and minutes later, James' leg was free.

"Stay clear of rubbish tips in future, James," said Sam. "They're full of hidden hazards."

"I will, Uncle Sam," said James.

Just then, Mike arrived. When he saw the boiler, he smiled. "That's just what we need, Sam," he said. "It's like this …"

Later on, Mandy heard steel band music. She looked out of her bedroom window and gasped in surprise. Sam was on Jupiter's platform and all her friends were outside, waving and dancing. Mike was playing a steel drum that Sam had made for him from what was left of the old boiler!

"**Wow!** It's just like the big carnival in Jamaica!" said Mandy, as her mum came into the bedroom.

"Yes," said Helen. "You can't go to Jamaica, so we brought the carnival to Pontypandy!"

"What are we waiting for, Mum?" said Mandy, happily. **"Let's dance!"**

Sam to the Rescue!

Poor Dusty! He's got his head stuck in the railings!
This is a rescue job for Fireman Sam! Can you show him
the quickest way through the maze to free Dusty?

Danger, Falling Sheep!

You can help read this story. Listen to the words and when you see a picture, say the name.

Norman

Mandy

James

Sarah

Woolly

Sam

Elvis

Penny

Tom

Dilys

One day,  is climbing

the mountain.  ,

and  watch him from the

ground. Suddenly,  falls

off a ledge and lands on  !

 sees  fall, and

calls  at the fire station.

Jupiter arrives with  ,

 and  .  looks

up. "I'll use the ladder to reach

 ," says  . But the

ladder is not long enough!

So  asks  to bring

the rescue helicopter.

 lowers a harness and

 puts it on. Then

swings  to the ledge

where  and  are

waiting. "Hold on, !" says

. "I'm coming."

puts the harness on  .

"Let's go, 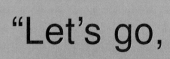," calls .

 grabs , then

 lifts  and

to safety. "You were so brave,

!" says . "

the Hero, that's me!" says

, grinning.

Back at home,  and

 have their dinner.

"  , where is your salad?"

asks  .  hears

a munching noise, and looks

under the table. Naughty

has given it to  !

Norman's Mountain Adventure

When Norman and Woolly got stuck on the mountain, Fireman Sam and the crew came to the rescue.

Tell the story of Norman and Woolly's adventure in your own words. The pictures will help you. Don't forget to make lots of **baa**-ing noises for Woolly!

①

Baaa!

Baaa!

2

Whoa!

3

Munch!

Norman's Invisible Friend

One day, Norman was watching a TV programme about a boy who had an invisible friend. **"Cool!"** he said. "I'd like one of those."

Later on, Norman met Sarah and James.

"Guess what?" said Sarah. "Bella gave us an ice cream for helping in the café."

"Did she now?" said Norman. That gave him an idea!

Norman went to the café and cleared the tables.

Bella was amazed! "Why – thank-a you, Norman!" she said. "That's-a so kind! You deserve-a an ice cream. 'Ere you are."

"Thanks!" said Norman. "Er ... can my new friend Owain have one too? He's too shy to come in."

Bella gave Norman another ice cream, and he went off licking **both** of them.

"Invisible friends come in very useful!" he said.

At the Flood house, Nurse Flood was getting things ready for Mandy's birthday party when she was called out on a job.

"Here's what you need to do," she told Mike, giving him a list. **"See you later!"**

The first guests were Sarah and James. Their present for Mandy was a popcorn maker.

"**Wicked!**" said Mandy. "Dad, plug this in, please!"

"Sure," said Mike. "I'll do the toasties as well."

Mike was in a bit of a flap! He didn't notice that he had too many things plugged into the adaptor. And he didn't notice that it was starting to smoke!

The children were upstairs when Norman arrived and put a pair of shoes under the coat rack.

"Whose are those?" said Mandy when she came downstairs.

"Er ... they're my new friend Owain's," said Norman. "He's in the bathroom."

"Oh," said Mandy. "Well, help yourselves to some food."

"I ... I mean ... **we** will," said Norman.

When Mike served up the food, Mandy sniffed. "I can smell burning, Dad," she said. "And now the smoke detector's going off!"

When Mike opened the kitchen door there was smoke everywhere! "Everybody out!" he said.

Mandy was on her way out when she saw Owain's shoes. "He must still be upstairs!" she told Sarah. "I'll go and get him."

Mike rang 999 and at the fire station, Elvis read out the emergency message. "There's a fire at Mike Flood's house!" he told the others.

"Action Stations!" said Station Officer Steele.

Sam, Steele and Elvis put on their helmets and jumped aboard Jupiter. The blue lights flashed, the siren wailed – Nee Nah! Nee Nah! – and they raced off. Penny was right behind them in Venus.

"Is everybody out?" Sam asked when they got to the house.

"No," said Sarah. "Mandy went upstairs to get Owain."

"Right," said Sam. "I'm going in!"

But as Sam went into the house, Norman stopped him.

"Owain isn't inside," he said. "He isn't anywhere. I made him up so I could get double helpings of things ..."

"But Mandy doesn't know that!" said Sam, going inside.

Sam soon found Mandy, and carried her downstairs. "But what about Owain?" she said.

"There is no Owain," said Sam. "Norman made him up."

When the fire was out, Sam explained what had happened. "You had too many things plugged into one socket, Mike." he said.

"I won't do it again, Sam," said Mike. "Now, let's carry on with the party at Bella's. Come on, Sam, Elvis, Penny, you're all invited."

At the party, Sam handed an empty glass to Norman.

"What's this?" asked Norman. **"Hey, where's my strawberry milkshake?"**

Sam grinned. "Your friend Owain must have drunk it!"

The Hero Next Door

Fireman Sam is always ready to help his neighbours.
He's The Hero Next Door!
Colour in his picture as neatly as you can,
using this one as a guide.
These are the colours you need:

blue

yellow

grey

black

red

brown

pink

Fit for Anything!

One morning, in the fire station gym, Station Officer Steele spoke to Sam. "I'm going to put you through your paces to see how fit you are," he said. "Firefighting is a tough job, and we need to be fit for anything!"

"Right, sir," said Sam. "Ready when you are!"

Steele looked at his clipboard. "Running on the spot first," he said. **"Begin!"**

Sam had only run a few paces when the alarm bell rang.

Elvis read out the teleprinter message. "Bella's cat is stuck up a tree in the park," he said.

"Action Stations, everyone!" ordered Station Officer Steele.

Sam, Steele and Elvis put on their helmets and jumped aboard Jupiter. The blue lights flashed, the siren wailed – **Nee Nah! Nee Nah!** – and they raced off.

When they got to the park, Sam put a ladder against the tree, and climbed up. He took Rosa in his arms, and carried her down to safety.

"My 'ero!" said Bella.

It was lunchtime when Sam and the others got back. Elvis made a big pan of spaghetti, but there was no time for Sam to eat any of it.

"Star jumps next!" said Steele. "Time him for ten minutes, please, Penny."

Sam did two star jumps – but then the alarm bell rang again.

"Sarah is locked in her bedroom," said Elvis. "She's stuck!"

"Action Stations!" said Station Officer Steele.

Sam, Steele and Elvis put on their helmets and jumped aboard Jupiter. The blue lights flashed, the siren wailed – **Nee Nah! Nee Nah!** – and they raced off.

When they got to the house, Sam jumped on to Jupiter's rescue platform, and was raised up to Sarah's window.

He lifted Sarah on to his shoulder, and carried her down to safety. **"Thanks, Uncle Sam!"** said Sarah.

It was three o'clock when Sam and the crew got back.

"Part three of your fitness test, Sam," said Steele.

But before Sam could begin, the alarm bell rang again.

"There's a house on fire in the High Street!" said Elvis.

"Action Stations!" said Station Officer Steele.

Sam, Steele and Elvis put on their helmets and jumped aboard Jupiter. The blue lights flashed, the siren wailed – **Nee Nah! Nee Nah!** – and they raced off.

As soon as they arrived, Sam unrolled the big, heavy hose and hauled it close to the house. Then he held it steady as water gushed out, and soon, the fire was out.

Back at the fire station, Sam went into the gym. "What's next, sir?" he asked.

Steele put away his clipboard. "I don't think we need to test your fitness, Sam," he said. "All the hard work you've done today proves that you are **fit for anything**!"

Hoses and Ladders

Play the Hoses and Ladders game with a friend. You'll need a counter each, and a die.

Put your counters on **START**, and take turns to roll the die. If you roll 2, move 2 spaces, and so on.

- If you land at the **bottom** of a **ladder**, climb **up** it.
- If you land at the **top** of a **hose**, go **down** it.
- If you land on a **badge**, have an **extra** turn.
- If you land on a **fire**, **miss** a turn.

The first player to reach **FINISH** is the winner.

20 FINISH

19

11

12

10

9

1 START

2

Good luck!

Mummy's Little Pumpkin

It was Halloween, and Dilys' shop window was full of paper ghosts, witches' hats and plastic bats.

She was building a display of cans on the counter when Norman came downstairs. **"Wooo!"** he wailed, creeping up behind her.

"Now just because it's Halloween, it doesn't mean you have to go scaring everyone, Norman," said Dilys.

"It does if you're the **Scariest Vampire in Pontypandy**!" said Norman.

Norman opened the door. "I'm off now!" he said. "Count Norman leaves in search of the biggest pumpkin in the world!"

Norman slammed the door behind him, and poor Dilys' display crashed to the floor.

"It's going to be one of those days!" moaned Dilys.

In the fire station garden, Sarah and James were helping Fireman Sam pick some pumpkins when Norman arrived.

"Looking for a pumpkin, Norman?" asked Sam, holding out a small one. "How about this one?"

Norman shook his head, and grabbed the biggest pumpkin. "This one's perfect," he said. "It's a **monster**, like me!"

Sam smiled. "I hope you're not going to scare everyone like you did last year," he said.

"Oh no, I won't do that again," said Norman. "This year I'm going to be **even scarier!**"

Back at the shop, Norman carved the pumpkin into a lantern. But he left the squishy bits of pumpkin on the floor, and when Elvis walked in, he slipped on them, and fell. **CRASH!**

Down came Dilys' display of cans again!

"Sorry, Elvis," said Dilys. "It's just one of those days."

"Can I light my lantern now, Mam?" asked Norman.

"I'll do it for you," said Elvis. "You've got to be careful with candles. **Always** ask a grown-up to light them, and remember to blow them out before you go to bed."

"OK," said Norman.

Later on, Dilys went upstairs. "Keep an eye on that candle," she told Norman, as he put the lantern in the shop window.

That night, Count Norman the Vampire opened the door and looked outside. **"Tremble with fear, Count Norman is here!"** he said, slamming the door and running off.

In the shop, the pile of cans fell off the counter again, and the pumpkin lantern rolled on to the floor. The candle inside fell over and the wax started a fire!

James and Sarah were in Bella's café when they saw the fire.

"Quick!" said Sarah. "We have to call Uncle Sam!"

At the fire station, Sam read out the emergency message. "There's a fire at Dilys' shop!" he told the others.

"**Action Stations!**" said Station Officer Steele.

Sam, Steele and Elvis put on their helmets and jumped aboard Jupiter. The blue lights flashed, the siren wailed – **Nee Nah! Nee Nah!** – and they raced off. Penny was right behind them in Venus.

Norman got home just as Jupiter arrived. "I'll save you, Mam!" he called to Dilys.

"Don't worry, Norman," said Sam, stopping him. "Leave it to us."

Elvis and Penny pointed a hose at the shop window, and Sam went up on the rescue platform. **"Hold on, Dilys!"** he said.

Sam lifted Dilys on to the rescue platform, and it was lowered safely to the ground.

"Thanks, Sam. **You're a hero**," said Dilys.

She gave Norman a big hug. "And so are you, Norman. You tried to save me. **You're Mummy's brave little pumpkin!**"

Everyone went into Bella's café, and Sam showed Norman what was left of his pumpkin lantern.

"Remember, Norman, always be very careful with candles, and put your lantern somewhere where it won't fall over," said Sam.

"And don't slam doors!" added Dilys.

"I won't, I promise," said Count Norman the Vampire. **"Happy Halloween, everyone!"**

Spot the Difference

There were lots of pumpkins to choose from in the fire station garden, but Norman wanted the biggest one!

1

These pictures look the same but
5 things are different in picture 2.
Can you spot them all?

2

The Case of the Missing Sweets

You can help read this story. Listen to the words and when you see a picture, say the name.

Dilys

Norman

Mandy

James

Sarah

Sam

Elvis

Penny

Dusty

 has a problem.

Someone is taking sweets

from the shop. "Is it you,

 ?" asks  .

shakes his head. "It's not me!"

says  .  and

set off to find the thief.

 did not take the sweets.

Neither did . "You need

to set a trap, ," says

. "I will!" says .

 puts some sweets on

the counter, then  and

 hide.

Suddenly,  sees smoke in

the shop. "**Fire!**" calls  .

 rings  .  ,

 and  arrive in

Jupiter and put out the fire.

Brave  rescues  .

"You're my hero!" says  .

Later on,  eats a biscuit.

 offers a bit to  .

But  doesn't eat it! "That's

funny!" says  . "

is **always** hungry! I wonder

what  has been eating

to make him full?"

Detective Norman knows who took the sweets now! Do you?
Yes, it was ... DUSTY, the sweet thief!

Naughty Dusty!
Woof, woof!

Safe at Last!

When Fireman Sam rescued Norman and Woolly from Pontypandy Mountain, they were cold and hungry, but safe at last! Which 2 pieces are missing from the jigsaw picture?

ANSWER: pieces b and d are missing.

Goodbye!

Nee Nah! Jupiter to the rescue! Colour in the picture as neatly as you can.